BASIL, the loneliest boy

JASON TIMLOCK
illustrated by
BRETT COLQUHOUN

Viking Kestrel

There was a very busy city
with lots of big buildings.

In the tallest building there were lots of apartments.

And in one small apartme[nt]
lived a boy named Basil.

He played on his own
because he couldn't go outside.

And he couldn't go outside
because it was not safe on his own.

Basil didn't know there were lots of other lonely children just like him.

They were lonely and
they were bored.
Nothing ever happened.

Until one evening Basil heard
a loud BOOM!
He ran out onto the balcony.

And all the other
kids did exactly
the same thing.

At exactly the
same time!

The twelve children watched from their balconies as fireworks exploded in the sky.

The twelve children waved happily to each other, until the fireworks stopped and they were called inside.

Basil wanted to play with the children.
The next day he thought of some ideas.

They tried sending notes along strings,

but the win
tangled the
strings.

They tried lots
of different things,

but nothing seemed
to work.

Then Basil made a poster and it said:

LET'S MEET
EVERY SATURDAY
MORNING AT
MY HOME AT
NINE O'CLOCK.
ASK YOUR
PARENTS.
LOVE BASIL.

And they did because:

twelve kids can swap toys,

twelve kids can go to the park,

and twelve kids can
have a party.

Thanks to Denise, Claire, Ryan, Jane and Maryann

Viking Kestrel

Penguin Books Australia Ltd 487 Maroondah Highway, PO Box 257 Ringwood, Victoria, 3134, Australia
Penguin Books Ltd Harmondsworth, Middlesex, England
Viking Penguin Inc. 40 West 23rd Street, New York, NY 10010, USA
Penguin Books Canada Limited 2801 John Street, Markham, Ontario, Canada, L3R 1B4
Penguin Books (N.Z.) Ltd 182-190 Wairau Road, Auckland 10, New Zealand

First published by Penguin Books Australia 1990 as *Basil, the loneliest boy in the block*

This US edition published by Viking Penguin Inc., 1990

Typeset in Cheltenham Book, by Leader Composition
Made and printed through Bookbuilders Ltd, Hong Kong

CIP

Timlock, Jason.
Basil, the loneliest boy.

ISBN 0 670 83125 5.

I. Colquhoun, Brett, 1958 – II Title.

III. Title: Basil, the loneliest boy in
the block.

A823' .3

The technique used is line drawing, coloured by plastic vinyl paint onto transparent acetate overlays.